Sins, Scars, and Second Chances:
Poems of Addiction and Recovery

Brett C. Persson

Sins, Scars, and Second Chances:
Poems of Addiction and Recovery
All Rights Reserved

X

@BrettCPersson

www.brettcpersson.com

This is a work of fiction. Names, characters, businesses, places, events, locales, and incidents are either the products of the author's imagination or used in a fictitious manner. Any resemblance to actual persons, living or dead, or actual events is purely coincidental.

Dedication

To those still lost in the darkness,
to the ones who have fought, fallen, and risen again.

To the souls trapped in the grip of addiction,
who feel there is no way out—
may you find the strength to take that first step.

To those who never made it out,
whose stories ended too soon,
you are not forgotten.

And to my family, who never gave up on me,
even when I had given up on myself—
this is for you.

02/01/2025

Dear Reader,

This book was never something I set out to write, but sometimes the past has a way of finding us. While going through old papers, notes, and journals, I came across a collection of unfinished poems—pieces of memories, raw emotions, and moments frozen in time. Some were nearly complete, others just scattered lines, but all carried a truth I couldn't ignore.

I decided to finish them.

These poems are a glimpse into my life, as well as the lives of others I have known—friends, strangers, and fellow souls lost in the grip of addiction. Some made it out. Others didn't. Their stories, my story, are all woven into these pages.

If you have never battled addiction yourself, I hope these words give you a deeper understanding of what it's like to live in that world. The chaos, the desperation, the fleeting highs, and the crushing lows. If you are in the grip of addiction right now, I hope you find something in these pages—a spark of courage, a whisper of grace, a reason to take that first step toward getting clean.

No one is too far gone. Hope is real. Recovery is possible.

Thank you for reading.

With gratitude,
Brett C. Persson

Table of Contents

The Edge of the Bottle, the Brink of the Grave

I drown in the silence of midnight's despair,
Where whiskey and sorrow hang thick in the air.
The weight of the bottle, the whispering haze,
Tells me I'm nothing, just counting my days.

The needle still calls with a voice like a friend,
Promising comfort, a means to an end.
But ghosts of my past, they rattle the door,
Begging me, pleading: Just die, or want more.

Sober's a mountain too jagged, too steep,
And who would I be if I woke from this sleep?
Would I face the wreckage, the bridges all burned?
Would I hate the man in the mirror returned?

But death, it is waiting, so easy, so near—
No shame, no struggle, no tremors, no fear.
A breath and it's over, the pain fades to black,
No cravings, no longing, no turning back.

Yet something still lingers, a flicker, a spark,
A whisper of hope in the grip of the dark.
What if there's more past the sickness, the fight?
What if I crawl from this pit into light?

The bottle still calls, the grave sings its tune,

But maybe, just maybe, I'll live past the ruin.

For death is forever, and maybe, just maybe,

Tomorrow holds something this nightmare can't take me.

First Sip at Twelve

The house slept heavy, shadows long,
A quiet night, but something wrong.
A whisper deep inside my head—
Go on, just one. No harm, no dread.

The cabinet stood, a secret shrine,
Behind its doors, a golden shine.
Bottles lined like whispered sins,
Each one daring me to begin.

My hands were small, but shook with thrill,
A reckless heart, a stolen will.
The cap unscrewed, the glass was poured,
A burning world I'd not explored.

First sip—too sharp, it seared my tongue,
A bitter bite, too old, too young.
Yet in that fire, something new—
A warmth, a buzz, a lighter view.

Laughter followed, soft and low,
A quiet joke only I'd know.
A secret safe within my chest,
A voice that swore, this feels like rest.

I never guessed how deep I'd sink,

How chains are built from just one drink.

But that night I learned, as most fools do,

That fire is warm—until it burns through.

Nights in Crisp Park

The streetlights hummed in the Florida heat,
Casting gold on the pavement beneath our feet.
A bottle passed between shaking hands,
Cheap and bitter, but we made our stand.

Crisp Park whispered in the dead of night,
A sanctuary bathed in half-lit light.
We laughed too loud, slurred our names,
Dared the world to call us tame.

The bay lay still, dark and wide,
A mirror for the ghosts inside.
Salt air mixed with whiskey's bite,
The stars blinked slow, too drunk for flight.

And there was Floyd, old and thin,
Wrapped in rags, soaked in gin.
He'd mutter stories, wild and bold,
Of lives he lived before he was old.

We listened, laughed, poured him some,
He grinned, said, "Boys, don't be dumb."
But wisdom's wasted on the young,
And we were gods with burning lungs.

Hours melted, time slipped past,

We chased the night, we drank too fast.

But in that park, we swore we'd stay,

Drunk on youth, too far away—

From knowing then what now is clear,

That those nights fade, but ghosts stay near.

Our Goodnight Saigon

We weren't students, just ghosts on the sand,
Two kids too young with drinks in hand.
Eckerd's lights flickered soft in the breeze,
The night was warm, the world at ease.

Chris poured beer into a plastic cup,
Laughed as the college kids filled them up.
We weren't their kind, but no one cared,
We drank like we belonged right there.

The bay stretched dark, waves whispered low,
The stars above put on their show.
We swayed to the rhythm of slurred delight,
No past, no future, just this night.

And when the bottles ran dry at last,
We staggered away, so drunk, night vast,
How fleeting youth, how quick it fades,
How soon the light betrays the shade.

Arm in arm, our voices bold,
We sang of battles fought and told.
"And we would all go down together,"
Echoed through the humid weather.

Chris laughed hard, I tripped, we swayed,

The car stood waiting, our minds frayed.

No war to fight, no enemy to meet,

Two lost youths, just roaming the street.

But time is cruel and nights grow thin,

And echoes fade where they begin.

We sang Goodnight Saigon on our way out,

Our youth trailing behind without a doubt.

Bathed in Gotham's Glow

The night buzzed electric, colors alive,
Neon streets seemed to twist and thrive.
Michael Keaton donned the cape,
My mind on a trip, illusion escape.

The theater swelled, dark and wide,
A portal yawning deep inside.
Lights went dim, the speakers roared,
Gotham rose, the madness soared.

Joker laughed, and so did I,
His painted grin stretched across the sky.
Smoke curled from the silver screen,
Every shadow pulsed between.

Batman swooped, cape like night,
A god of vengeance, sharp and bright.
His cowl, his glare, his silent breath—
I swore I stood an inch from death.

Gotham spun in shades unknown,
Buildings melted, faces shone.
The Batmobile streaked like fire,
My pulse raced—higher, higher.

Somewhere deep inside the haze,

I lost the line between the plays.

Reality flickered, danced, then bent—

Was I here, or just my mind spent?

And when the credits rolled at last,

I staggered out, the moment passed.

The city hummed, the streets still glowed—

But Gotham stayed, and I still rode.

High at the Altar, Bound by Love

Nineteen years old, heart in a race,
Dressed in white, she shined with grace.
Hands clenched tight, vows to be sworn,
A ring, a promise, a life reborn.

Cocaine burned behind my eyes,
Numb and wired, lost in the highs.
Fear like thunder, loud and real,
A child, a wife, too much to feel.

The preacher spoke, the words blurred fast,
The future loomed, the past a blast.
Was I a man, or just a child,
I looked at her, just smiled.

Kim's eyes locked, steady, bright,
A beacon cutting through the night.
Her voice was calm, her love was true,
She held me up, she never knew.

A breath, a pause, a whispered "Yes,"
A trembling hand, a soft caress.
Through fear and doubt, through wasted days,
She stayed, she loved, she led the way.

Now years have passed, and love still stays,

Through broken nights and brighter days.

The boy who feared, the man who grew,

Found strength in love, found life in you.

One Bullet, One Breath

The bottle was low, the day stood still,
Whiskey burned hot, but I drank my fill.
The walls closed in, oh so tight,
A storm of silence, no more fight.

A loaded gun, cold in my hand,
A deadly game, a line in the sand.
One spin, one click, a hollow prayer,
Breath held tight in the desert air.

The barrel kissed my trembling skin,
A dare, a dance, a fight within.
Would fate be kind, or call my bluff?
Darkness grew, life felt so rough.

'Click'

The sound was sharp, a ghostly voice,
A whisper questioning my crazy choice.
I poured another, let it drown,
The weight of all that pulled me down.

I dropped the gun, I hit the floor,

A drunken wreck, a man no more.

And Kim, her love, her steady grace,

Would never see this hollow place.

The night still held me, thick and black,

But something told me—don't look back.

Kinsey Took the Wheel

The sun hung high, too bright to bear,

My breath was thick with hops and air.

The bottle lay empty the thirst still burned,

No way to stop, no lesson learned.

"Come on, Kinsey," I held out the keys,

She froze, uncertain, like a breeze.

Thirteen years, too young to drive,

But I was drunk—we'd both survive.

She'd steered before on dust and dirt,

Five acres wide, no risk, no hurt.

But pavement stretched beyond our land,

And still, I placed the wheel in hand.

The engine hummed, she gripped it tight,

The world ahead too sharp, too bright.

I leaned back, half asleep,

While she stayed sober, driving deep.

Through streets and the passing cars,

She kept us straight, ignored the scars.

No laughter came, no childish thrill,

Just fear that sat too hard, too still.

She pulled up slow, let out a breath,

A child aged beyond her depth.

I bought my beer, my selfish sin,

Blind to her stress, all about the win.

Now time has passed, and still, I feel—

The day my child took the wheel.

Through the Glass, Through the Shame

The floor swayed hard, my legs gave out,
Too drunk to stand, too gone to doubt.
I meant to piss, to make it right,
But balance slipped into the night.

One step, one sway, the world let go,
Then through the glass, a crashing blow.
The shower door gave way to me,
A drunken wreck, a fool set free.

No blood was spilled, no wounds to see,
Just shattered pride surrounding me.
Kim came running, fear in tow,
Her voice was sharp, her eyes were low.

"Are you hurt?" she asked, still there,
But in her face, just worn-out care.
I laughed, I swore, I waved her off,
A king still ruling through a cough.

A saint with a patient hand.
She sighed, and helped me stand,
No words were said, no fight was thrown,
Just silence heavy, sharp as stone.

And though the glass was swept away,
The cracks it left would always stay.

Drunk on the Mic, Lost in the Song

The TV glowed, the music swelled,
A drunken king, a stage upheld.
The Wii remote, my microphone,
A living room turned concert throne.

Kim just laughed, the kids did too,
As I belted notes I never knew.
Slurring words, off-key and loud,
I swayed before my captive crowd.

"Don't stop believin'!"—I gave it all,
Stumbled, tripped, but stood up tall.
A rockstar in a beer-soaked haze,
Lost in Idol, lost in praise.

The kids took turns, their voices bright,
While I kept drinking through the night.
Kim rolled her eyes but sang along,
A chorus drowning all the wrong.

And though my score was barely there,
And though my pitch was past repair,
For just one night, without a doubt,
I sang my heart completely out.

Beer, Headlights, and the Cow That Lived

The road stretched long, the night was black,
A bottle deep, no turning back.
Windshield blurred, hands unsteady,
Foot too heavy, mind not ready.

The cooling towers loomed ahead,
Ghosts in the dark, cold and dead.
No cars, no lights, no signs of life,
Just me, the wheel, full of strife.

Then—eyes like lanterns, wide and bright,
A sudden shape in pale moonlight.
A beast stood dumb, the world stood still,
A moment stretched, a frozen thrill.

Too late to swerve, too late to pray,
The brakes screamed loud, the tires gave way.
Steel and flesh, a fate so thin,
One breath more and I'd have crashed in.

The cow just stared, calm as the sky,
As if to ask, "Will you live or die?"
Then slowly turned, walked past my door,
And left me drunk, alive once more.

I sat there, hands still white with fear,

A fool who danced too close, too near.

No witness watched, no sirens wailed,

Just heavy silence, as my fear trailed.

The road was empty, dark and wide,

But luck had chosen not to collide.

Two lives still standing past that day,

The cow moved on, I drove away.

Line in the Pisser

Stall door creaked, neon buzzed,
Hands unsteady, heartstrings fuzzed.
Pocket dug deep, bag torn wide,
White dust spilled where filth resides.

A curse, a sigh, a desperate scan,
No table, no sink—just porcelain tan.
The urinal stared, a mocking throne,
But waste not, want not—I was alone.

Key to my nose, no shame, no pride,
One deep breath, the rush inside.
The stench was foul, the burn was quick,
But craving won—I took my pick.

The world snapped bright, a lightning crack,
Ego surged, no looking back.
Did it matter? Did I care?
What's dignity when highs are rare?

Mirror glance, eyes too wide,
A king of nothing, lost in pride.
A public stall, a desperate game,
One more line, one more shame.

The Sound of Madness (And THX)

The bottles clinked, the night felt right,
A buzz so thick, the world felt light.
Wires tangled, speakers stacked,
Surround sound finally unpacked.

A final plug, a simple click,
Then came the sound, so loud and thick.
A rising hum, a thunderous roar,
THX shook the house to the core.

I laughed too loud, eyes open wide,
"This is it! Come on inside!"
The kids rolled eyes, groaned in pain,
"Dad, not again! It sounds the same!"

But no, they're wrong—it had to play,
Again, again, ten times that day.
I cranked it up, I made it last,
It echoed deep, the speakers blast,

Kim just sighed, walked away,
The kids swore they'd move someday.
Yet there I stood, lost in sound,
THX shaking all around.

The night wore on, the beer ran dry,

At last, I yawned, let silence lie.

But in my heart, I swear it's true—

That sound was magic, crisp and new.

The Meeting

Fluorescent lights hum soft and low,
Folding chairs in a patient row.
The coffee's strong, burnt and thin,
A bitter start for those who sin.

The room feels heavy, stories untold,
Eyes that have seen both young and old.
A hush, a nod, a knowing glance,
A seat is found—a second chance.

A man stands up, voice worn but sure,
"No crosstalk here, let's keep it pure."
He clears his throat, begins to say,
"Welcome to A.A. today."

A prayer is spoken, words well-known,
A quiet hope in voices grown.
Then page is turned, the book is read,
Twelve simple steps for lives once dead.

The silence thick, the air runs tight,
Then one by one, they share their fight.
Their voices crack, their hands may shake,
But still, they speak, they will not break.

And in this room, no past is banned,

No soul too lost to take a stand.

For here, in pain, we seek the light—

One day sober, one more night.

Hope in Recovery

The nights were long, the road was dark,
I chased a high, I lost my spark.
The bottle lied, the needle burned,
Each bridge behind me left unturned.

But deep inside, beyond the pain,
A voice remained, a faint refrain.
A whisper small, a steady light,
That dared me stand, that fought the night.

he hands of strangers pulled me near,
Their voices steady, calm and clear.
"Keep coming back," they said, they swore,
"One more day, then one day more."

So step by step, I learned to stand,
To trust the world, to reach a hand.
To trade the lies for something true,
To let the past fade out of view.

Hope is not a perfect road,
Not free of storms, not lightly stowed.
But in this fight, I've come to see,
That hope was always here in me.

White Fire and False Relief

A line so fine, the razor glides,
Two powders mixed, the darkness hides.
Cocaine sparks, it burns so bright,
Oxy soothes, it drowns the fight.

A breath, a rush, a sudden flight,
My heart beats wild, my chest turns tight.
Cold sweat drips, the room expands,
A god, a ghost with trembling hands.

Euphoria hums, my mind is wide,
The world dissolves, I float inside.
No pain, no past, no need to feel,
Just velvet waves, so sharp, so real.

But highs betray, and time runs thin,
What lifts me up will pull me in.
A fleeting throne, a king's disguise,
Yet every reign must end in lies.

The crash comes hard, my hands go numb,
The ringing fades, the demons come.
One more line, one last reprieve,
A game I play, but can't believe.

I chase the burn, the cold embrace,

But in the mirror—just my face.

A hollow man, a vacant stare,

Still snorting dreams that lead nowhere.

Drunk in the Lights of Rocky Horror

The city roared, the night was bright,
Neon buzzed in electric light.
A kid too young, a flask in hand,
Stumbling streets I barely planned.

New York pulsed, a fevered dream,
I swayed through crowds, lost in steam.
Theaters called, their doors swung wide,
A cult of misfits trapped inside.

"Let's do the Time Warp!"—voices screamed,
Fishnets flashed, the sequins gleamed.
A world unchained, a stage set free,
But booze had wrapped its chains on me.

The walls leaned first, or maybe I,
The floor rose up to meet my side.
Sliding slow, the world went thin,
The laughter blurred, the lights caved in.

I sat there drunk, a grinning fool,
A kid too lost to play it cool.
The movie played, the people danced,
And I just drowned in circumstance.

New York pulsed, the lights burned bright,

The credits rolled, dissolving night.

I swayed, I stumbled, found my feet,

A drunken shadow on the street.

Port-a-Potty Peril

Stumbling drunk, I had to go,
The beer had filled me head to toe.
A port-a-potty stood in sight,
A beacon in the dim moonlight.

I yanked the door, near lost my grip,
The floor was rocking like the ship.
Sat down? No way! I stood with pride,
Unzipped my jeans and aimed inside.

But fate, my friend, had set a trap,
A cruel, unholy bathroom slap.
The seat was down—I didn't see,
Till warm regret came splashing me.

A golden wave, a wicked tide,
Soaked my legs from thigh to side.
I jumped, I cursed, I spun around,
Feet now slipping on the ground.

The smell rose up, so sharp, so vile,
My dignity lost in rank denial.
No way to fix it, no way to hide,
Just piss-stained jeans and wounded pride.

I staggered out, the cool air hit,

My friends just laughed—I had to quit.

Lesson learned, a drunken woe:

Check the seat before you go!

A Father's Pride, A Son's Redemption

His voice was strong, steady, clear,
The words I'd longed my whole life to hear.
"I'm proud of you," he said at last,
And every failure, every past—

Fell away like dust in the breeze,
Replaced by something sure and free.
The weight I'd carried, the shame I'd known,
Faded in the love he'd shown.

He'd never wavered, never turned,
Through all my wreckage, all I'd burned.
A steady man, my guiding light,
Through darkest days, through endless nights.

And now at last, I stood up tall,
No longer lost, no chance to fall.
His pride in me, mine in him too,
A bond once cracked, now strong and true.

I met his eyes, no words were said,
But in his gaze, my past had fled.
A father's love, so fierce, so bright,
Had led me back into the light.

Step Four: The Mirror of Truth

I walked the path, the steps began,
But now I faced the hardest stand.
A fearless search, a deep review,
Of all I'd done, of all I knew.

The past lay waiting, raw and wide,
No place to run, no place to hide.
Resentments burned, regrets ran deep,
The wounds I'd caused, the ones I keep.

Each page I filled, each line confessed,
Revealed the weight upon my chest.
The lies I told, the trust I broke,
The hurt I left in words I spoke.

But in the dark, the light was near,
Each truth I wrote dissolved my fear.
No longer chained by guilt and shame,
I owned my past, I spoke my name.

Step Four had cut, it had revealed,
But in the pain, I'd learned to heal.
For only through the past's review,
Could I begin to start anew.

Blackout Nights, Forgotten Days

The bottle tipped, the night grew wild,
I laughed too loud, I cursed, I smiled.
The world spun fast, then spun some more,
As I stumbled through the open door.

The clock had vanished, time was gone,
The night stretched out, yet felt all wrong.
A ghost inside my hollow frame,
Lost in a night I couldn't name.

Did I dance? Did I fight?
Did I vanish in the night?
Did I call? Did I cry?
Did I swear I'd say goodbye?

The morning sun, too sharp, too bright,
Cuts through the wreckage of last night.
Bruised up knuckles, aching head,
Unknown places, a strangers' bed.

The questions rise, the answers fade,
A life misspent, a price unpaid.
Each blackout night, a borrowed breath,
A step too close to meeting death.

But one day came, the bottle fell,
I woke to face my private hell.
No longer lost, no longer blind,
A sober chance, a clearer mind.

The War Within

The battle starts before the dawn,
Another day, the past drags on.
The mirror shows a hollow face,
A life once full now lost in space.

The cravings whisper, sharp and low,
"Just one more time, no one will know."
My hands still shake, my body aches,
Each promise made just bends and breaks.

The past still knocks, it calls my name,
It pulls me back into the flame.
The memories sting, the guilt runs deep,
Dark secrets buried, scars to keep.

The nights stretch long, the days move slow,
The weight of pain won't let me go.
Yet somewhere deep, a voice still cries,
"Keep holding on, just one more try."

Through sweat and shakes, through shattered pride,
Through all the times I swore, I'd died.
One step, one breath, I rise, I heal,
The chains once tight begin to peel.

The war still rages, never done,

Each fight is hard, but battles won.

Yet hope now shines where darkness bled,

A life reborn, a past now shed.

From Ruin to Redemption

Upon the edge of death's embrace,
He walked alone, devoid of grace.
A hollow man, a tattered soul,
Consumed by vice, beyond control.

The bottle ruled, the needle lied,
Each fleeting high, a slower slide.
The days were blurred, the nights were black,
No way ahead, no turning back.

His hands had stolen, lips had sworn,
His heart was heavy, stained and worn.
Through empty streets, through wasted years,
He drowned in guilt, he choked on fears.

But in the dark, a whisper grew,
A voice he lost, yet somehow knew.
It called him soft, it called him near,
"There's more to life than pain and fear."

He fell, he wept, he cursed the sky,
"Why save me now? Just let me die!"
But mercy's light would not depart,
It burned within his broken heart.

A stranger found him in the dirt,

With hands outstretched to heal the hurt.

"Come with me, son, and take my hand,

There's hope ahead, there's solid land."

A weary nod, a trembling start,

A step toward grace, a change of heart.

Through sweat and pain, through sleepless nights,

He faced his past, he faced the fight.

Each tear he shed, each wound laid bare,

Unraveled knots of deep despair.

And through the war, through every scar,

He found a strength beyond the bar.

One day, one breath, the chains fell free,

The man he was, he used to be.

The thirst was gone, the hunger died,

A soul once lost, now sanctified.

And in the place where ruin stood,

A life rebuilt, a heart turned good.

He found his faith, he walked in light,

No longer slave to endless night.

Now strong and steady, standing tall,

He lifts the lost so they won't fall.

His scars now speak of where he's been,

A light to guide the lost within.

Sold for a Fix

She walks the streets, the neon cold,
Her body's young, her soul feels old.
A ghost wrapped up in skin too tight,
Another deal, another night.

Her arms are track-marked, bruised and thin,
The price she pays to chase the sin.
Each promise fades, each high runs dry,
She swears she'll quit, she swears she'll try.

The men don't care, they never ask,
She plays the part, she wears the mask.
A hollow smile, a painted face,
Another stranger, same embrace.

A crumpled bill, a motel key,
A life reduced to currency.
She trades herself, she sells her name,
For one more hit to numb the shame.

But somewhere deep, beyond the pain,
A whisper fights against the chain.
A voice she knew, a time before,
When life was worth a little more.

She stares into the bathroom glass,

A broken past, a time gone past.

She lifts the phone, a call to make,

A final step, a chance to take.

One breath, one tear, one silent plea,

A prayer for strength, for dignity.

Tonight's the night, she turns the page,

To break the chains, to leave the cage.

Three Doors at the End

The road was long, the nights were black,
Each fix, each high, no turning back.
He swore he'd stop, he swore he'd try,
But every vow was just a lie.

The needle called, the bottle sang,
A hollow voice, a metal fang.
Through burning veins, through poisoned breath,
He danced too close to fate and death.

Yet time runs thin, the choices fade,
And three doors stand where games are played.
No other paths, no other way,
Just where the wasted end their days.

Jail—the first, cold steel and stone,
A nameless face, a life alone.
Bars replace the streets he knew,
A cage built high, no sky in view.

Institution—white walls so bare,
Lost inside a hollow stare.
Strapped down tight, his mind unwinds,
A prisoner now of his own mind.

And Death—the final, darkest door,

Where silence falls forevermore.

No second chance, no time to plead,

Just one last breath he'll never need.

He walks the line, but fails the test,

A soul enslaved, a life possessed.

For all who chase the dragon's breath,

The road will end in bars or death.

Nothing Wasted

He wakes in shakes, his body sore,
Yet reaches for the drink once more.
The bottle tips, his hands unsteady,
The thirst too deep, the sickness ready.

He drinks too fast, he drinks too much,
A burning flood, a deadly crutch.
His stomach turns, his body groans,
A drowning man in seas unknown.

The sickness comes, he bends in pain,
Yet even now, he won't refrain.
He heaves, he gags, he spits, he chokes,
Yet nothing here will be a joke.

A colander waits upon the floor,
A trick he's used so long before.
The chunks stay back, the liquid flows,
And where it goes, he surely knows.

He lifts the bowl with shaking hands,
No shame, no choice, no other plans.
A sip, a gulp, the fire remains,
It soothes his soul, it numbs his veins.

The mirror calls, but he won't see,

The hollow ghost he's come to be.

For nothing's left, yet still he tries,

To wring the last drop from his lies.

Fifteen Minutes of Forever

The lines were thick, the rush was fast,
A jolt so strong, I knew won't last.
But something twisted, something turned,
A fire inside, too bright, too burned.

My heart kicked hard, too fast, too wild,
Feeling scared and full of fear, like a child.
My breath came short, my chest locked tight,
A dizzy fall, a fading light.

"Oh God, oh shit, this might be it,"
I clenched my fists, show my grit.
The walls closed in, the room spun wide,
No place to run, no place to hide.

Each second crawled, each thought grew worse,
A heartbeat cursed, a racing hearse.
I swore I'd change, I swore I'd pray,
Just let me live another day.

Then slowly, softly, like a tide,
The panic ebbed, the storm untied.
The pulse came down, the world stood still,
Fifteen minutes bent my will.

I wiped my face, I shook my head,

Still here, still high, still not quite dead.

Yet deep inside, I knew too well,

One more night, and this could be hell.

But fear is fleeting, gone too fast,

A lesson learned that doesn't last.

The clock struck two, my hands still shook,

Yet there I stood, another look.

The powder lay in perfect lines,

A lure too strong, a trap designed.

I told myself, *"Just one, stay cool,"*

Then sniffed away my fear like a fool.

LSD & Liquor Store Schemes

The ceiling swirled, the walls turned bright,
No sleep would come, not on this night.
My mind ran wild, my thoughts took flight,
A liquor store locked in my sight.

Just down the street, a neon glow,
A place where all the good drinks flow.
I laid in bed, my plan was tight,
A perfect crime before first light.

The register—quick, grab the cash,
The cameras—small, a simple dash.
The bottles lined up, stacked with care,
I'd take my pick, no time to spare.

A shadow fast, a silent creep,
No trace left when I made my leap.
The clerk would freeze, too scared to shout,
Before he knew, I'd be back out.

But as I planned, the walls caved in,
The colors danced upon my skin.
Was this a thought or some disguise?
Were schemes just dreams behind my eyes?

For hours long, I worked it through,

Each step, each turn, each thing to do.

But when the sun began to rise,

I laughed and blinked at clear blue skies.

Still in bed, still high, still free,

Just me, my thoughts, my LSD.

No crime was done, no cash was stacked,

Just madness spun that led me back.

Stolen Days, Shattered Nights

They roam the streets with hollow eyes,
Hearts gone cold from years of lies.
No job, no home, no place to stay,
But hunger drives—it won't delay.

A watch, a wallet, a purse, a ring,
Anything turns to the fix they bring.
A stranger's trust, a friend's last loan,
All just fuel to chase the stone.

Car doors checked in dim-lit lots,
Breaking locks for what they've got.
Pawn shop deals, a quick exchange,
A cycle deep, a life deranged.

Mom's old TV, Dad's old gun,
Another hit, another run.
No shame, no thought, no looking back,
Just one more high to fill the lack.

Police lights flash, but they don't care,
A junkie's life is stripped down bare.
Jail's just time till they get out,
And steal again without a doubt.

A habit built on blood and theft,

Until there's nothing, no one left.

And in the end, the choices fade—

A cell, a grave, or change be made.

The Lost and the Light

Through midnight streets he stumbled slow,
A hollow man with nowhere to go.
His breath was sharp, his steps unsure,
His body weak, his soul impure.

The neon flickered, cold and bright,
A city drowning in the night.
His pockets empty, veins run dry,
A ghost beneath the weeping sky.

Each alley whispered, each bar called,
But in his chest, his heart had stalled.
No more to steal, no more to sell,
His world had sunk too deep in hell.

Then through the dark, a voice rang clear,
A tone so calm, yet rich with fear.
"My son, you walk a broken road,
Lay down your sins, release your load."

A man in robes, a cross held tight,
A priest who stood beneath the light.
His eyes were kind, yet burned with fire,
A warmth that cut through cold desire.

"You've lost your way, but not your soul,
For even now, you can be whole.
You chase the pain, you drown in sin,
Yet Christ still calls—He'll take you in."

The addict laughed, his lips curled tight,
"You think your God can stop this fight?
I've bled, I've begged, I've sold my name,
There's nothing left but guilt and shame."

The priest stepped close, his gaze held strong,
"You've carried this for far too long.
The path you walk, it leads to death,
But grace can save your final breath."

A trembling sigh, a shaking head,
The addict dropped to knees of lead.
For years he'd run, for years he'd fought,
Yet mercy stood where once was not.

The priest knelt down, his voice so low,
"Just say His name, and He will know.
Repent, my son, and let Him see—
The broken man who longs to be free."

With one last tear, with one last sigh,
He raised his hands up to the sky.
"Oh God, I'm lost, I've gone too far,
Yet here You stand, despite my scars."

A light so soft, yet fierce and bright,
Seemed to cut into the night.
The weight he bore began to fade,
A soul once lost, no longer strayed.

Through midnight streets he walked no more,
No ghosts to chase, no bars, no score.
For in the dark, where sin had reigned,
A spark of grace, a soul reclaimed.

Giving Back, Staying Strong

The road was dark, the nights were long,
But somehow, still, I carried on.
Through shattered days and wasted years,
Through drowning pain and hollow fears.

But now my hands reach out, not take,
No more lies, no more fake.
Clean and sober, here I stand,
To serve, to heal, to lend a hand.

In halls where sorrow fills the air,
I sit with those who know despair.
I tell my tale, they tell me theirs,
A bond of pain, a hope we share.

I see the ghosts behind their eyes,
The dreams they lost, the endless lies.
Yet in their tears, I see a spark,
A chance to rise beyond the dark.

For every word I give away,
A piece of me is saved today.
Each story shared, each hand I hold,
Keeps my own heart from growing cold.

We walk together, step by step,
One more day, one more rep.
For when we serve, we start to see,
That saving them is saving me.

Thank You, Bill W.

I walked through fire, I lost my way,
Drowned in bottles, night and day.
I swore I'd stop, I swore I'd try,
Yet every drink became a lie.

But through the haze, a light still shone,
A path laid down, I wasn't alone.
A man who knew, who'd lived the same,
Who gave his hope, who spoke my name.

Bill W., your words rang true,
A lifeline strong, a guide brand new.
Twelve simple steps, twelve doors to grace,
A way to heal, to find my place.

Because of you, I stand today,
One day sober, come what may.
Your gift still echoes, far and wide,
A fellowship, a strength inside.

So here's my thanks, both loud and clear,
For showing us there's hope right here.
A life once lost, now whole and free,
Bill W., you saved me.

The Weight of the Trigger

I sat alone, the engine hummed,
A loaded past, a future numb.
The cold steel pressed against my lips,
A trembling hand, a tightened grip.

They knew it all, the lies, the shame,
The broken trust, the hollow name.
The weight of failure, thick as stone,
The kind that sinks, the kind that owns.

I feared the road that lay ahead,
The fight, the pain, the words unsaid.
The restless nights, the demons near,
The echoes loud, the doubt, the fear.

How could they stand to look at me,
A man unmade, too blind to see?
A son, a husband, father, friend,
Now just a wreck too far to mend.

One pull, one flash, it all would cease,
No rehab steps, no slow release.
No whispered talks, no judging eyes,
No waking up to long goodbyes.

But as I sat there, steeped in doubt,

The coward in me won the bout.

Too scared to go, too lost to stay,

Yet one more breath still found its way.

I dropped the gun, I met the dawn,

Another chance, another wrong.

A road not taken, a fight unplanned,

Yet here I was, still in demand.

The weight remained, but so did I,

A broken man who chose to try.

For in my fear, in all my pain,

The choice to live still had my name.

A Prayer for the End

I whispered low with shaking breath,
"Oh Lord, just grant me peaceful death."
No strength to fight, no will to stand,
Just let me slip from this cruel land.

The bottle's grip, the needle's sting,
Had stripped away my everything.
Each promise broke, each hope betrayed,
A life once whole now torn and frayed.

I begged for mercy, begged to go,
To leave behind this endless woe.
For in my mind, the cure was clear—
No life, no pain, no need to fear.

Yet silence held, no answer came,
Just one more night inside the flame.
And through the dark, though faint and weak,
A voice still called, too soft to speak.

It did not judge, it did not blame,
It did not curse my tarnished name.
It whispered slow, so calm, so deep,
"This war's not yours alone to keep."

So though I prayed for death that night,

I woke again to morning light.

And in that breath, though frail, unsure,

A hint of hope began to stir.

From Shadows to Light

The world was bright when I was young,
Yet shadows crept where songs were sung.
A boy unbroken, bold and free,
But whispers called and tempted me.

At first, a taste, a fleeting thrill,
A moment's rush, a bending will.
What harm, I thought, could pleasure bring?
Just one more sip, just one more fling.

The years went by, the chains grew tight,
The days blurred into endless night.
A hollow man with hollow eyes,
Lost in the haze of whispered lies.

I ran, I fell, I lost my way,
A storm of sorrow, dark and gray.
Each promise made was quick to break,
Each step I took, a grave mistake.

Through shattered glass and wasted years,
Through nights of doubt and hidden tears,
Through prison walls of my own mind,
I searched for hope but none to find.

Then came the day—the breaking ground,

The moment when the truth was found.

No lie could mask the mirror's stare,

No way to hide the vacant glare.

The walls closed in, my breath was tight,

I stood upon the edge of night.

A voice inside, both fierce and small,

A whispered cry, a final call:

"Enough, enough, the time is now,

No more to drink, no more to bow.

The road is long, the fight is rough,

But in your heart, you are enough."

With trembling hands, I took a stand,

Let go the bottle, let go the hand

Of demons who had danced with me,

And sought the path to being free.

The first steps burned, the hunger screamed,

My body shook, my spirit beamed.

The poison gone, the mind laid bare,

Yet in the pain, I found a prayer.

Each dawn, a battle yet to fight,

Each dusk, a whispering of light.

One day, one breath, one step at last,

The future built upon the past.

And by my side, her steady grace,

Her patient hands, her loving face.

Through every storm, through every fall,

She held me firm, she gave her all.

With love, I rose, with love, I healed,

With love, my purpose was revealed.

Not just to live, but now to lead,

To plant in others hope's small seed.

No chain remains, no fear, no doubt,

The fire within has not burned out.

I stand with men, I raise my voice,

For every soul must make their choice.

The road ahead still winds and bends,

Yet through the storm, my heart ascends.

Not just for me, but those behind,

The weary hearts, the burdened mind.

For if my tale can light the way,

Then let it shine, then let it stay.

A beacon bright for those who roam,

To guide them to a life called home.

No chains remain, no bars, no fears,

No drowning sorrow, wasted years.

For I am free, my soul has grown,

Through love and strength, I have atoned.

And in the morning's golden gleam,

I live, I lead, I dare to dream.

Living Without Regret

The past still whispers in the night,
A ghost that lingers, pale and slight.
It weaves its tales of days long fled,
Of words unsaid, of tears once shed.

I've walked through fire, lost in haze,
Through broken nights and wasted days.
I've carried shame, I've bowed to doubt,
I've wondered if I'd make it out.

But time moves on, it does not wait,
The clock won't pause to barter fate.
Regret, a weight upon the chest,
A cruel thief who robs my rest.

Yet what is done cannot be chased,
No pages torn, no lines erased.
The ink has dried, the tale is told,
But still, the heart can turn to gold.

For in the wounds, a lesson lives,
And in the dark, the dawn forgives.
The past was mine, yet not my chain,
Each scar a map, not just a stain.

I do not walk with head held low,

I do not drown in what I know.

The road ahead is wide and bright,

And I will fill it with the light.

No backward steps, no shame to keep,

No endless night, no dreamless sleep.

I choose to stand, I choose to be,

A soul unshackled—finally free.

So let the past remain the past,

A teacher's voice, a lesson cast.

I'll write today with steady hands,

And build a life that understands.

For every breath, a brand-new page,

A chance to heal, to turn the stage.

No more regret, no debt unpaid,

Just love, just hope, a life remade.

The Power of Sobriety

I walked the road of ruin deep,
Where shadows danced and demons creep.
A bottle clenched within my fist,
Each sip a step to the abyss.

The nights were long, the dawns were gray,
Each promise broke by light of day.
Regret would rise with morning's glare,
Yet still, I drank, I didn't care.

I chased relief in poison's tide,
Yet found no peace, just hollow pride.
The faces blurred, the laughter died,
And all I loved was cast aside.

I swore I'd stop, I swore in vain,
Yet drank to numb the growing pain.
A prisoner bound by liquid chains,
Trapped in the past, lost in remains.

Through heavy doors, I made my way,
Unsure of what my lips would say.
A circle formed, a chair stood bare,
I took my place, breathed the air.

A stranger spoke, yet told my tale,

A life once wrecked, a path once frail.

Their words rang true, their eyes held grace,

And for the first time, I felt a place.

"One day at a time," the wisdom rang,

A melody the lost ones sang.

A chant of hope, a steady guide,

A force that stood where fear once lied.

The steps were clear, the path was laid,

A debt to settle, wounds to fade.

No longer lone, no longer blind,

I found a home, a hand, a mind.

The first was hardest, raw and real,

A reckoning I feared to feel.

The weight of past, the wreckage wrought,

The guilt, the shame, the battles fought.

Yet as I spoke, the chains uncoiled,

The years of lies, the love I'd spoiled.

Each tale confessed, each burden shed,

Each whispered hope where once was dread.

Through nights of doubt, the war was waged,

Through cravings fierce, through tempers caged.

Yet I endured, yet I survived,

And in the fire, I revived.

And in these rooms, I saw the light,

In others' eyes, in battles a fight.

The broken men, the shattered wives,

Rebuilding love, reclaiming lives.

Where once was rage, now laughter grew,

Where once was loss, the dawn broke through.

A father's tears, a mother's grace,

A child held in a firm embrace.

The homes rebuilt, the friendships mended,

The wasted years, at last, transcended.

Where poison ruled, now wisdom stays,

A life remade in sober days.

Through work, through a guiding hand,

We lift the lost, we help them stand.

For once like them, we knew the cost,

The aching soul, the moments lost.

But now we stand, with heads held high,

No longer bound, no longer lie.

A drink? No more—it holds no power,

For we have bloomed, we've reached our hour.

And now I walk with strength anew,

A guiding light for those still blue.

For every soul that longs for air,

I stand, I speak, I show I care.

Not just for me, but all who seek,

The weary lost, the bruised, the weak.

For in these rooms, the truth still thrives,

And in these steps, we save our lives.

A day will come, I do not doubt,

When grief will rise, when fear will shout.

But I have learned, through loss and pain,

That from the drink I must abstain.

One step, one breath, one guiding prayer,

A fellowship beyond despair.

For in this life, I stand anew,

And live with hope—because of you.

Chaos in the High

The night was thick with rage and smoke,
A drunken laugh, a twisted joke.
The pills were gone, the bottle dry,
Yet tempers flared, no reason why.

A shove too hard, a word to start,
A fist that struck, a breaking heart.
The glass went flying, a voices screams,
The air was thick with shattered dreams.

Paranoia, fire and fear,
Blinded eyes that once were clear.
A friend, a brother, lost in haze,
Now just strangers set ablaze.

Sirens wail, the blue lights spin,
The wreckage of what once had been.
Blood on knuckles, tears on skin,
Another night where none will win.

And when the dawn begins to rise,
They'll wake with pain and hollow eyes.
Regret will whisper, truth will sting,
Yet still they'll chase the same old thing.

The Ruin at the Table

The room was warm, the voices light,
A family gathered, fearing a fight.
Laughter echoed, plates stacked high,
But in my haze, it passed me by.

My hands unsteady, eyes too wide,
A restless storm I could not hide.
I cracked a joke, my laugh too strong,
Their faces fell—I'd got it wrong.

A reckless rant, a slurred-out cheer,
Soft whispers spoke of shame and fear
A mother's sigh, my father's stare,
A brother's shake, a cousin's glare.

I spilled my drink, I cursed, I swayed,
The laughter died, the smiles strayed.
My brother stood, my uncle frowned,
Yet still, I spoke, I doubled down.

Another scene, another fight,
Another ruined family night.
I swore I'd leave, I slammed the door,
The road outside would hear me roar.

But in the dark, when high ran thin,

The shame came creeping back within.

A wreck, a fool, consumed by shame,

A life once bright, now lost in flame.

And though they loved me, stood so near,

Each gathering grew cold with fear.

A table set, my seat still there,

Yet all I brought was pain to share.

The Hollow Inside

I wake to shadows, thick and deep,
A world that spins, yet I can't keep.
Each breath is heavy, thick with doubt,
A whisper soft, *"You won't climb out."*

The needle calls, the bottle sings,
A siren's song with poisoned strings.
I reach, I take, I drown, I fade,
Lost inside the mess I made.

Regret's a ghost I cannot flee,
It lingers deep inside of me.
No matter where I choose to stray,
My past still finds me on the way.

They say there's hope, they say there's light,
But all I see is endless night.
I chase relief, I beg, I pray,
Yet nothing ever seems to stay.

My hands still shake, my body's sore,
Trapped in mistakes I've made before.
Too tired to run, too weak to fight,
Hopelessness becomes my night.

Only by Giving

I walked this road, I know it well,

The highs, the lows, the taste of hell.

I've felt the chains, I've begged, I've bled,

I've wished at times that I were dead.

But hands reached out, they pulled me through,

From darkest nights to skies of blue.

They gave me hope, they showed the way,

And now it's mine to give away.

For if I hold this gift too tight,

Its fragile flame will lose its light.

But when I give, when I let go,

The light inside will only grow.

So take my hand, I've stood where you stand,

I know the weight, I understand.

One step, one breath, we'll make it through,

What saved my life can now save you.

Trapped in the High

I wake to shakes, my body screams,
Another day of broken dreams.
No food, no rest, no peace, no pay,
Just one more hit to start the day.

I swore I'd stop, I swore I'd change,
But cravings whisper, voices strange.
"Just one more time, then you'll be free,"
But every time, it buries me.

My hands go numb, my mind's a haze,
The nights blur into endless days.
I steal, I lie, I sell my name,
A life reduced to chasing flame.

The faces fade, the love won't stay,
Alone I watch them walk away.
The world moves on, the clock ticks fast,
Yet here I sit, still chained to glass.

The highs feel good, but never last,
Each crash is harder than the last.
A hollow ghost, I stand, I sway,
Too lost to leave, too scared to stay.

The mirror cracks, I meet my stare,
A stranger's eyes are looking there.
Is this my end? Is this my fate?
Or can I turn before too late?

Facing the Mirror

I walked in slow, my head held low,
A place where I had feared to go.
No more lies, no more disguise,
Just broken dreams and bloodshot eyes.

The walls were plain, the air was cold,
The weight of truth felt hard to hold.
No bottles near, no pills to chase,
Just me, my past, and my disgrace.

They spoke of hope, they spoke of pain,
Of lives rebuilt, of hearts unchained.
But all I saw was what I'd done,
The bridges burned, the battles won.

The nights I missed, the tears I caused,
The wreckage left in all my flaws.
The faces faded from my view,
Of those who cared but now withdrew.

Yet day by day, I found my voice,
I stood, I spoke, I made a choice.
To face my past, to stand up tall,
To own my wrongs, to take the fall.

No road is smooth, no path is straight,

But change begins when we don't wait.

And though my past will always stay,

I choose to walk a different way.

Kim's Love, My Light

Through drunken nights and hopeless days,
She stayed beside me, lost in haze.
Through every lie, through every fall,
She held on tight—she loved through all.

Her voice was steady, soft yet true,
She saw my worst, but still pulled through.
While others turned and walked away,
She knelt and fought for me to stay.

The nights I vanished, lost in haze,
The broken vows, the empty days.
She wiped my tears, endured the pain,
Yet through it all, she still remained.

She prayed for hope, she prayed for light,
She prayed I'd make it through the night.
And when I fell, too lost to stand,
Her love reached out, a steady hand.

It wasn't rage, it wasn't fear,
Just quiet faith that brought me here.
She saw the man I'd failed to be,
And fought to bring him back to me.

Now clean and strong, I've found my way,

Because she chose to always stay.

Her love held firm, through darkest skies,

And through her love, I rose to rise.

Gone Too Soon

He walked with fire, he chased his dreams,
A mind so sharp, built strong with schemes.
A partner, friend, a man so bold,
But now his story won't be told.

Just thirty years, so full of drive,
A future bright, yet not alive.
He played the game, he risked the cost,
One night too much, and all was lost.

She woke beside him, reached to feel,
But found a touch so cold, unreal.
Her cries rang out, her heart fell still,
A life cut short by a tiny pill.

No warning call, no last goodbye,
Just silent walls that asked her why.
A ring still worn, a love still true,
Yet nothing left that she could do.

The world moves on, but scars remain,
A widow's loss, a friend's deep pain.
And though he's gone, his fate still speaks,
The cost of highs brings endless weeks.

So now I stand, I walk the line,

I hold his name, I keep it mine.

For in his fate, the truth is plain,

Some roads bring light, some end in pain.

The Man in the Alley

Through shadowed streets he walked alone,
A king without a lasting throne.
His crown was glass, his scepter flame,
His kingdom built on loss and shame.

The needle called, the bottle sang,
Each whisper soft, yet sharp with fang.
He chased the highs, ignored the lows,
A life reduced to fleeting throes.

His mother prayed, his father cried,
They watched their son dissolve inside.
A wife once swore to see him through,
But love can break when lies are true.

He tried to fight, he swore he'd change,
Yet every vow fell out of range.
He walked through doors of shaking hands,
But left before the meeting stands.

One step, two steps, then he fell,
Each day a slow descent to hell.
Hope flickered, faint, but could not grow,
For chains held tight where light won't go.

He begged for time, he swore once more,

But fate had locked a final door.

A needle kissed his weary skin,

A bitter love, a cold within.

The city hummed, the streetlights glowed,

Yet none would see his life erode.

No friends remained, no voices cried,

No hands to hold him as he died.

And there he lay, in alley deep,

The world still turned, he fell to sleep.

A nameless man, a fleeting breath,

A soul consumed, a lonely death.

For some will fight, and some will win,

And some are lost to what's within.

The battle rages, fierce and wide,

But not all make it to the other side.

Sixteen and Lost

The night was cold, the air was thin,
A young man's heart beat fast within.
Sixteen years, so lost, so wild,
A broken soul, no longer a child.

His hands were numb, his mind was dark,
A hollow hunger left its mark.
The cravings burned, the need was strong,
A voice that whispered, *"Just go along."*

A liquor store, a cash-filled till,
A simple job, a fleeting thrill.
A gun held tight in shaky hands,
A life undone by poor demands.

The door swung wide, the bell gave sound,
The clerk looked up, then quickly frowned.
A father first, his stance was still,
Two kids at home, a house, a will.

"Just give it up," the young man said,
The clerk just sighed and shook his head.
"You don't have to, son—just walk away,"
But sixteen knew no other way.

A shot rang out, the silence broke,

The smell of powder, dust, and smoke.

The father fell, his story done,

A final breath, a setting sun.

A scream behind—too late, too fast,

A customer had heard the blast.

She turned to run, but fate was set,

A second shot—the same regret.

Two lives now gone, the register full,

Yet still, the hunger held its pull.

The money clutched, the drugs would flow,

But blood will stain where greed will grow.

The sirens wailed, the lights drew near,

The young man stood, consumed by fear.

The rush was gone, the thrill had passed,

Only ruin left at last.

The cell was cold, the bars were tight,

No moon to shine, no guiding light.

At sixteen years, his fate was sealed,

A wasted life, a grave revealed.

Two children mourn, a widow cries,

A mother prays with hollow eyes.

For in one night, with fleeting gain,

He bought his high, but lost his name.

The Red Light Reaper

The night was dark, the road was slick,
His hands unsteady, breath too thick.
The whiskey burned, the wheel turned fast,
A race with fate he'd never last.

The speedometer climbed, the lights flew by,
A drunken king beneath the sky.
No thoughts of risk, no fear, no shame,
Just one more mile in fortune's game.

A red light glowed, a final chance,
But through the fog, it failed to dance.
His foot pressed hard, the tires cried,
A fleeting chance, now cast aside.

Across the way, a family rode,
A mother humming, hearts bestowed.
A father smiled, his hands held tight,
Two little souls bathed in moonlight.

Their laughter stopped, a flash, a sound,
A world once whole, now split and bound.
Metal crumpled, screams rang wide,
Four souls lost in fate's cruel tide.

His car spun out, the road grew still,

His hands went limp, his breath was nil.

No time for guilt, no chance to plead,

Just silence left where pain would breed.

The papers read, *"Five now dead,"*

A reckless man, a fate he spread.

No second chance, no words to mend,

A drunken ride, a bitter end.

Lost Souls in the Grip of the Game

They wander streets with hollow eyes,
Chasing ghosts in midnight skies.
Their hands once strong now shake with need,
A life consumed by endless greed.

The needle calls, the bottle sings,
A lullaby with poisoned strings.
Each hit, each sip, a fleeting high,
Yet every road still leads to die.

Their families wait, their loved ones cry,
Yet all they do is bleed and lie.
They sell their past, they steal their name,
Just players in a losing game.

The mirror shows a face unknown,
A shadow lost, a heart of stone.
They swore they'd stop, they swore they'd try,
But every vow was just a lie.

Some fade away in jails so cold,
Some never make it to grow old.
Some rest beneath a nameless grave,
Still trapped inside the highs they crave.

Yet somewhere deep, beyond the pain,

A voice still whispers, soft but plain:

"You're not too lost, you're not past hope,

There's still a way for you to cope."

The Road to Redemption

I walked through fire, I walked through pain,
Chased the highs, but found the chain.
The needle lied, the bottle burned,
Each turn I took, the wrong I turned.

The nights were endless, cold and black,
Regret was all that had my back.
I stole, I lied, I lost my way,
A soul too lost to kneel and pray.

Yet in the dark, a whisper grew,
A voice so soft, yet strong and true.
"This life you're living isn't done,
There's still a way, there's still the sun."

I clenched my fists, I cursed the sky,
I swore I'd quit—another lie.
But something changed, I can't say why,
A spark still burned, refused to die.

One step, one breath, one shaking start,
A battle waged inside my heart.
Through nights of torment, days so long,
Through voices pulling, sharp and strong.

But then the morning felt so new,

The weight had gone, the sky turned blue.

No longer chained, no longer weak,

A voice inside began to speak.

I found the light, I found my grace,

A sober life, a brand-new place.

No longer lost in endless need,

No longer bound to pain and greed.

Now laughter rings where silence grew,

The ones I hurt, they saw me through.

The past still lingers, wounds run deep,

But hope is mine, it's mine to keep.

For though the road was hard and steep,

The climb was worth the soul to keep.

And now I stand, both strong and free,

A life reclaimed—*the best of me.*

11/14/11